LITTLE

WOLF

Written by **Teoni Spathelfer**

Illustrated by Natassia Davies

HERITAGE

Heritage House Publishing Company Ltd.
heritagehouse.ca

Cataloguing information available from Library and Archives Canada

ISBN 978-1-77203-347-2 (cloth)
ISBN 978-1-77203-380-9 (paperback)
ISBN 978-1-77203-348-9 (ebook)

Cover and interior book design by Jacqui Thomas

The interior of this book was produced on FSC®-certified, acid-free paper,
processed chlorine free and printed with vegetable-based inks.

Heritage House gratefully acknowledges that the land on which we live and work is within the
traditional territories of the Lkwungen (Esquimalt and Songhees), Malahat, Pacheedaht,
Scia'new, T'Sou-ke, and W̱SÁNEĆ (Pauquachin, Tsartlip, Tsawout, Tseycum) Peoples.

We acknowledge the financial support of the Government of Canada through
the Canada Book Fund (CBF) and the Canada Council for the Arts, and the
Province of British Columbia through the British Columbia Arts Council
and the Book Publishing Tax Credit.

25 24 23 22   2 3 4 5

Printed in Canada

I Giaxsixa/thank my Mom

and our ancestors

for leading the way.

To my three brilliant daughters,

Desiree, Orielle, Sage,

and to my four amazing grands,

Cole, Kara, Summer, and Deacon,

always honour your journey.

I am blessed to be your Mom and Dede ♥!

You all make our ancestors so proud!

Thank you to Johnny for asking,

"How do you always spot wildlife

everywhere you go?" ♥

When her parents separated, Little Wolf, her sister, and their mother moved from the country to a big city. The city was busy and noisy and made of concrete. Little Wolf felt as though she didn't belong there. She dreamed of living in the country again, surrounded by a forest and animals.

"Little Wolf" was the spirit name she secretly gave herself so that she could stay strong in the city's jungle. In the heart of the city, on one of its busiest streets, Little Wolf would sit on the front steps of her grandmother's house. She would howl at the full moon when she longed for the smell of the forest. This animal song brought a smile to her heart.

Since she was a baby, Little Wolf had a lazy eye. But this never stopped her from spotting a chickadee in a tree at the big park in her neighbourhood or an owl under a bridge. When she and her mom and sister took the bus out to the farmlands to visit her cousins, Little Wolf always looked for hawks on fence posts and herons hunting in the fields for mice.

One day, her cousin asked her how she always spotted wildlife everywhere she went.

Little Wolf said, "I look for the thing that is different on the land or in the ocean, and the thing that is different is usually an animal."

The city where Little Wolf lived was surrounded by a
long sea wall. Little Wolf loved walking along the sea
wall because she could look down into the water and spot
otters. One early spring day, she put on her favourite red
rain jacket and set out on her walk. As she searched the
shoreline, an otter started swimming alongside her!

Little Wolf made sure she wore her red jacket every
time she walked along the sea, so the otter could pick her
out from the other people. The otter found her all that
spring, and they wandered along happily together on
many days. Finding nature in the city made Little Wolf
feel happy and more at home.

The other kids at Little Wolf's school were from many cultures, but no one else was Indigenous, like her. One day at recess, a large group of students surrounded Little Wolf and said mean things to her because of her heritage. They called her bad names. She was afraid, and those few minutes seemed to last forever.

Little Wolf didn't know what to do or say to the kids. Suddenly, she found herself howling at the top of her lungs. Her wolf song made the mean kids go away!

Little Wolf's mom wanted her to feel good about her culture, so once a week they went to beading class together. Little Wolf loved the smoky smell of the tanned moose and deer hide that they sewed beads onto. She also joined a traditional West Coast dance class, where she could pretend that the whole world was her dance floor!

Little Wolf's mom told her stories about their family, who have lived on their territory for over fourteen thousand years. She told Little Wolf that their people are Ocean People. They have been making beautiful, sturdy canoes for as long as anyone can remember. Little Wolf loved learning what her ancestors ate, how her people still caught their own food, and how they entertained one another around a warm fire at night, telling stories of challenge, victory, and love. Little Wolf learned that her own grandfather wrote songs that were performed during traditional ceremonies.

Every summer Little Wolf looked forward to going fishing with her grandfather. He would sell his salmon catch, and once he reached the limit he was allowed to sell, Grandpa would catch salmon for his family, their village, and relatives living in the city. Little Wolf loved to eat the salmon jerky her Nanny made. Even when she ate it in the cold of winter, it reminded her of summertime.

Her absolute favourite part of going on Grandpa's fishing boat was seeing the swift, magical dolphins that would swim and leap beside their boat! As long as the dolphins were swimming with them, Little Wolf would forget to help Grandpa on the boat. She would smile for hours as the dolphins played. Grandpa didn't mind. He loved seeing his granddaughter so happy.

Back in the city, when Little Wolf thought about her dolphin friends, she would move her arm up and down like the waves they swam through. Whenever she had a dream about swimming with her summer dolphins, she would wake up happy!

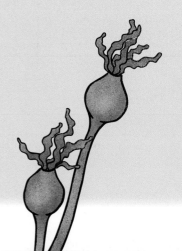

Little Wolf's mom knew how much she loved to be outdoors, so on her tenth birthday they took the bus to go get a surprise birthday present.

"This present will help you get outdoors on the sunniest of days and the coldest of days," her mom said.

Little Wolf couldn't wait to find out what it was.

They stopped in front of a building, and Little Wolf could hear dogs barking inside. It was a shelter for animals that needed new homes.

They went inside and looked at all the dogs that could be adopted. There were big fluffy dogs, tiny dogs that didn't eat very much food, old dogs, and puppies.

It was hard to choose which dog would be best for her family, until she got to the last cage. There stood a quiet and friendly dog with shaggy, multicoloured fur. He licked Little Wolf's hand and sat on her feet and looked up at her with big, pretty eyes. This was the one she chose. She named him Prince and loved taking him for walks in the sunshine and the cold. This was her favourite birthday present of her entire life!

At school, things were getting a bit easier. Little Wolf loved going to her school library and reading about people from all over the world. One day she read a sad book about Black people who were once enslaved. The book was written by a wise man named Martin Luther King Jr., who wanted peace for people of all colours. His words inspired Little Wolf and made her feel hopeful.

Little Wolf grew older and more confident and graduated from elementary school. She was nervous about starting high school, but also excited. Her mom took her shopping for school clothes, and Little Wolf chose a white long-sleeved t-shirt with colourful pictures of girls from different cultures. There was even an Indigenous girl on the shirt. Little Wolf loved this shirt. She wore it with pride and had her school picture taken in it!

Although she lived away from her traditional territory, and would travel to far away places throughout her life, Little Wolf was always proud of her heritage.
It was a part of her, like the wolf song in her heart.

SAGE MAZZOTTA

Teoni Spathelfer is a member of the Heiltsuk Nation from coastal BC. Since childhood she has loved immersing herself in her own culture and learning about other cultures around the world. Spathelfer is the author of the Little Wolf Series (*Little Wolf*, *White Raven*, and *Abalone Woman*) for young readers. She has worked as a publicist; a radio journalist, host, and producer; and an arts and music writer. Her documentary *Teoni's Dream*, informed by her mother's residential school experience, has aired nationwide on CBC Radio. Her photography has been featured across various media and sold privately. She has been blessed with three daughters and four grandchildren. She lives in Sooke, BC.

Natassia Davies is an artist and graphic designer of Coast Salish ancestry. She is the illustrator of the Little Wolf Series, by Teoni Spathelfer. For nearly a decade, Davies has worked traditionally and digitally to create illustrations, develop visual brand identities, and design various other visual communications tools for local businesses, individuals, and non-profits. She also works with other First Nations Peoples and Indigenous groups to create educational tools and public art pieces. Davies has collaborated on multiple large-scale Indigenous murals that can be found throughout Sooke and Victoria's harbour.